Goblin Sharks

by Grace Hansen

Abdo Kids Jumbo is an Imprint of Abdo Kids
abdobooks.com

abdobooks.com

Published by Abdo Kids, a division of ABDO, P.O. Box 398166, Minneapolis, Minnesota 55439. Copyright © 2021 by Abdo Consulting Group, Inc. International copyrights reserved in all countries. No part of this book may be reproduced in any form without written permission from the publisher. Abdo Kids Jumbo™ is a trademark and logo of Abdo Kids.

Printed in the United States of America, North Mankato, Minnesota.

052020
092020

 THIS BOOK CONTAINS RECYCLED MATERIALS

Photo Credits: Alamy, AP Images, BluePlanet Archive, Granger Collection, iStock, NHPA/Photoshot, Science Source

Production Contributors: Teddy Borth, Jennie Forsberg, Grace Hansen
Design Contributors: Dorothy Toth, Pakou Moua

Library of Congress Control Number: 2019956562

Publisher's Cataloging-in-Publication Data

Names: Hansen, Grace, author.

Title: Goblin sharks / by Grace Hansen

Description: Minneapolis, Minnesota : Abdo Kids, 2021 | Series: Spooky animals | Includes online resources and index.

Identifiers: ISBN 9781098202521 (lib. bdg.) | SBN 9781098203504 (ebook) | ISBN 9781098203993 (Read-to-Me ebook)

Subjects: LCSH: Goblin shark--Juvenile literature. | Sharks--Behavior--Juvenile literature. | Marine fishes—Behavior--Juvenile literature. | Curiosities and wonders--Juvenile literature.

Classification: DDC 596.018--dc23

Table of Contents

Goblin Sharks 4

Food 18

Baby Goblin Sharks 20

More Facts 22

Glossary 23

Index 24

Abdo Kids Code 24

Goblin Sharks

Goblin sharks live throughout the Atlantic, Pacific, and Indian Oceans. They spend most of their time in the deep sea. Because of this, they are rarely seen.

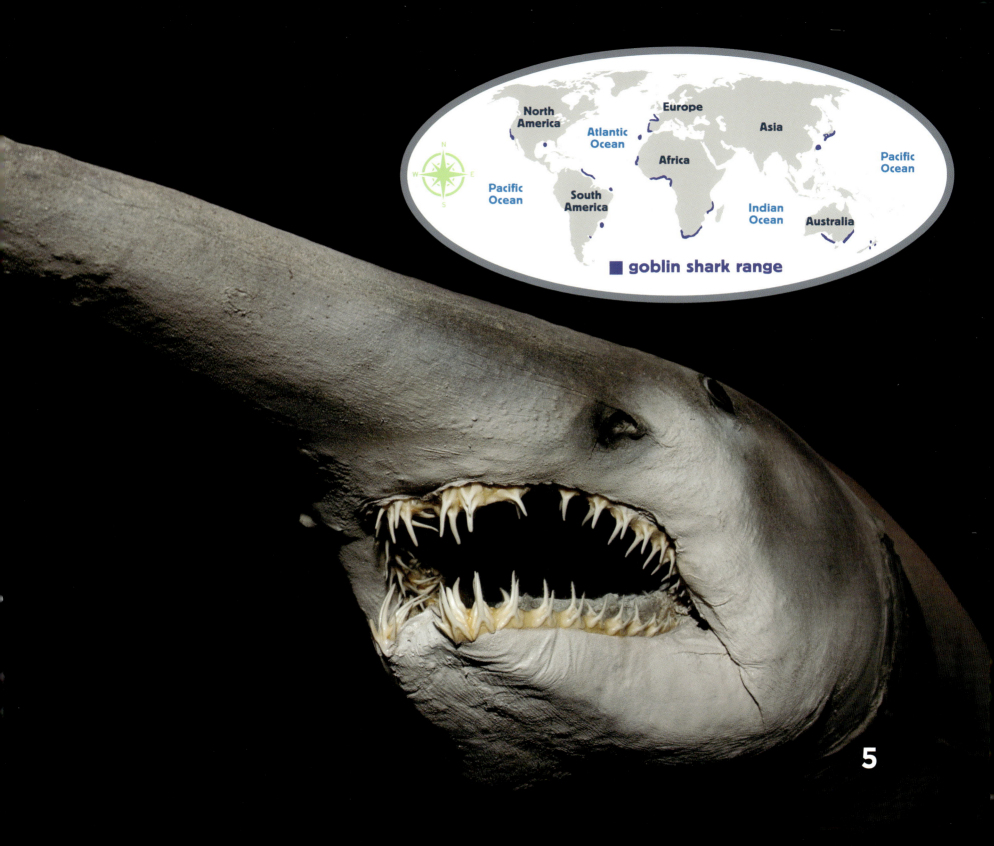

Most goblin shark sightings have taken place off the coast of Japan. These sharks look a lot like goblins that appear in Japanese **folklore**. This is how they got their name.

Goblin sharks are just plain scary looking! Their bodies are soft and saggy, but large. They can grow to be 12 feet (3.7 m) long and 460 pounds (209 kg).

A goblin shark is pinkish in color. This is because its skin is nearly see-through. The pinkish hue is from its **blood vessels**.

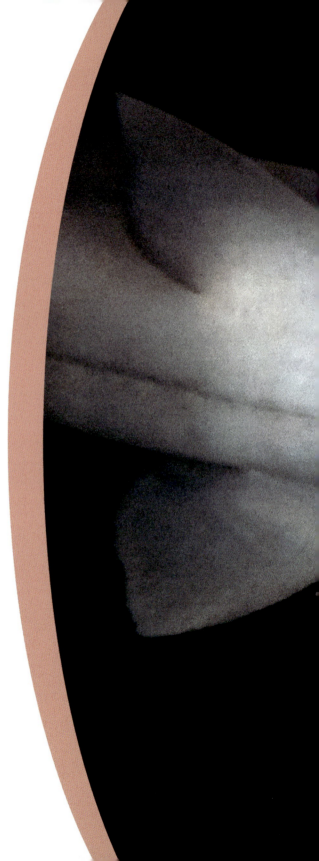

Goblin sharks have long, flat **snouts**. Their snouts are called rostrums.

A goblin shark's rostrum is very **sensitive**. The shark uses it to find **prey** in its deep, dark habitat.

15

The goblin shark also has rows of fang-like teeth. Its jaw can thrust 3 inches (7.6 cm) out of its mouth. This is how goblin sharks catch their prey.

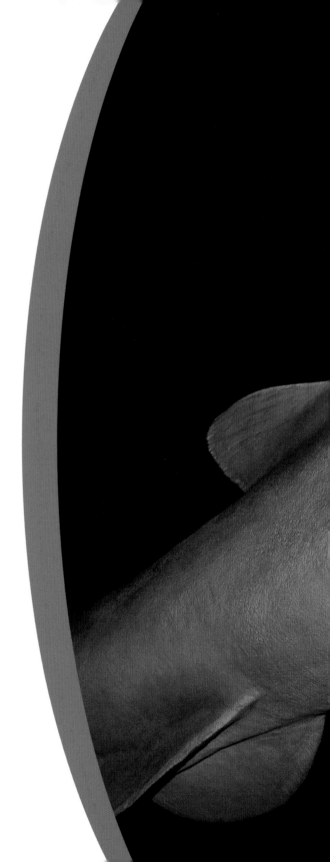

17

Food

Goblin sharks like to eat bony fish, squid, and **crustaceans**. They probably eat in deep water or near the seafloor.

Baby Goblin Sharks

Scientists do not know much about goblin shark **breeding**. Females give birth to a small number of young. Newborn goblin sharks are able to hunt right away.

21

More Facts

- Goblin sharks can live at least 4,200 feet (1,280 m) below the ocean's surface.

- Teeth in the back of the goblin shark's mouth are smaller. The shark uses these teeth to crush its prey.

- Goblin sharks cannot fit all of their teeth into their mouths. This makes them look extra spooky!

Glossary

blood vessels – thin tubes in the body through which the blood moves.

breeding – the act or process of making young.

crustacean – an animal, like crabs and lobsters, with a hard jointed shell.

folklore – the stories and ways of a group of people from a certain place or country.

prey – an animal being hunted by another animal for food.

sensitive – able to sense things very well.

snout – the front part of an animal's head that sticks out.

Index

Atlantic Ocean 4

babies 20

body 8

color 10

food 14, 16, 18

habitat 4, 14

hunting 14, 16, 20

Indian Ocean 4

Japan 6

mouth 16

Pacific Ocean 4, 6

size 8

skin 8, 10

snout 12, 14

teeth 16

Visit **abdokids.com** to access crafts, games, videos, and more!

Use Abdo Kids code **SGK2521** or scan this QR code!